Dear Parents:

Congratulations! Your child is taking the first steps on an exciting journey. The destination? Independent reading.

STEP INTO READING® will help your child get there. The program offers five steps to reading success. Each step includes fun stories and colorful art or photographs. In addition to original fiction and books with favorite characters, there are Step into Reading Non-Fiction Readers, Phonics Readers and Boxed Sets, Sticker Readers, and Comic Readers—a complete literacy program with something to interest every child.

Learning to Read, Step by Step!

Ready to Read   Preschool–Kindergarten
• big type and easy words • rhyme and rhythm • picture clues
For children who know the alphabet and are eager to begin reading.

Reading with Help   Preschool–Grade 1
• basic vocabulary • short sentences • simple stories
For children who recognize familiar words and sound out new words with help.

Reading on Your Own   Grades 1–3
• engaging characters • easy-to-follow plots • popular topics
For children who are ready to read on their own.

Reading Paragraphs   Grades 2–3
• challenging vocabulary • short paragraphs • exciting stories
For newly independent readers who read simple sentences with confidence.

Ready for Chapters   Grades 2–4
• chapters • longer paragraphs • full-color art
For children who want to take the plunge into chapter books but still like colorful pictures.

STEP INTO READING® is designed to give every child a successful reading experience. The grade levels are only guides; children will progress through the steps at their own speed, developing confidence in their reading.

Remember, a lifetime love of reading starts with a single step!

For Benjamin and Malcolm
—V.S.

Visit us on the Web!
StepIntoReading.com
randomhousekids.com

For more information on Disney Infinity, please visit Disney.com/Infinity

Educators and librarians, for a variety of teaching tools, visit us at RHTeachersLibrarians.com

ISBN 978-0-7364-3427-0 (trade) — ISBN 978-0-7364-8244-8 (lib. bdg.)
ISBN 978-0-7364-3428-7 (ebook)

Printed in the United States of America 10 9 8 7 6 5 4 3 2 1

Disney INFINITY

READY TO PLAY!

by Victoria Saxon

illustrated by Erik Doescher

Random House 🏠 New York

"What is this place?"

Hiro exclaimed.

He and Baymax looked around.

They had been transported

to a strange new world

by a shooting star.

"It's like a big toy box," Hiro said.

"Here come the toys," Baymax said.

An army of zurgbots
was marching toward them.
They were coming from a castle
in the distance.

"Duck!" someone shouted.

Hiro turned to see a girl

carrying a bow and arrow.

He bent down

as she raised her bow.

She shot three arrows.

One, two, three bots fell!

But more bots kept coming.

"I'm Merida," she said.

"Let's go."

"Baymax," Hiro said. "Stop them!"

Baymax launched his rocket fist.

It smashed through the bots.

Hiro used his microbots

to make a wall.

"Why are they attacking us?"
Hiro asked.

"They're defending the castle,"
Merida said.

"Who's attacking the castle?"

Hiro asked.

Merida held another arrow to her bow.

"*We* are," she said.

She explained that the villain Zurg

had captured Aladdin!

He wanted Aladdin's magic lamp.

Suddenly, a large man roared,

"I'm gonna wreck it!"

Wreck-It Ralph ran out from the trees.

He swung his huge fists

and smashed several bots.

A princess named Jasmine
arrived on her magic carpet.
She kicked and twirled,
creating a magical sandstorm.
The bots were swept away.

"Let's get to the castle,"

Jasmine said.

"Zurg has trapped Aladdin inside."

They raced to the castle.
Zurg appeared at the top
of a tower.
He had made a giant maze
to block the entrance.

"You must find Aladdin
before time runs out,"
Zurg announced.

Hiro, Jasmine, and Merida

prepared to race through the maze.

Hiro told Ralph and Baymax

to guard the entrance.

"You can fight off any bots

that try to follow us," he said.

Merida went first.

Jasmine and Hiro went next.

SWOOSH! SWOOSH! SWOOSH!

They dodged the swinging hammers.

Next, they leaped
through rings of fire.
Then they jumped
from one moving pad
to another.

"I'll be back," Merida said.
She slipped under the floor
and disappeared.

"Mwa-ha-ha!" Zurg laughed.

"Aladdin is doomed!"

"You'll never get past this!"
Zurg told Jasmine and Hiro.
Several elevator platforms began
to rise and fall in front of them.
Hiro and Jasmine sprang
from one platform to another.

Hiro and Jasmine climbed
until they reached the top
of the wall.

Zurg stopped laughing.
He turned and fled
into the castle.

Jasmine and Hiro followed Zurg.

They found him with Aladdin.

Aladdin was trapped

in a force field!

"Tell me now!" Zurg demanded. "Where did you hide the lamp?"

Aladdin refused to speak.

Jasmine threw a sword
to Aladdin.
He sliced through
the force field.
He was free!

"Tell me now!" Zurg demanded.

"Where did you hide the lamp?"

Aladdin refused to speak.

Jasmine threw a sword
to Aladdin.
He sliced through
the force field.
He was free!

Zurg was furious!

He tried to attack them.

Hiro trapped Zurg

with a wall of microbots.

"Follow me!" Aladdin said

to his friends.

"I hid the magic lamp on the roof."

Hiro and Jasmine ran after him.

Aladdin grabbed the magic lamp.

Zurg's bots and guards charged.
Aladdin raised the magic lamp
and zapped some of them.
But there were too many!

"Give it to me!" Zurg said.

Suddenly, a cherry bomb landed
next to Zurg.

KABOOM!

Ralph had scaled the castle walls.

Baymax and Merida were with him.

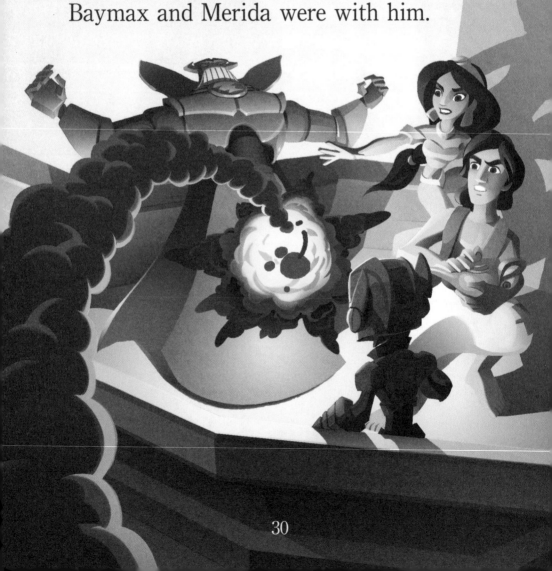

"Get him!" Merida cheered.

Baymax launched his rocket fist.

It knocked Zurg off the castle!

Everyone cheered.
Zurg was defeated,
and Aladdin was free.
Their adventure was over,
but more adventures
were sure to come!